PmS

Dirty Bertie

FAME!

For David ~ D R

For Cameron and Ben ~ A M

STRIPES PUBLISHING
An imprint of Little Tiger Press
1 The Coda Centre, 189 Munster Road,
London SW6 6AW

A paperback original
First published in Great Britain in 2016

Characters created by David Roberts
Text copyright © Alan MacDonald, 2016
Illustrations copyright © David Roberts, 2016

ISBN: 978-1-84715-666-2

Printed and bound in the UK.

10 9 8 7 6 5 4 3

Dirty Bertie

FAME!

DAVID ROBERTS WRITTEN BY ALAN MACDONALD

Collect all the Dirty Bertie books!

Contents

CHAPTER 1

Bertie plodded downstairs. He could hear his parents talking in the kitchen.

"That was Miss Lavish from the drama group on the phone," said Dad. "She says a company are looking for boys to come to an audition."

"For a play?" said Mum.

"No, it's something on TV," said Dad.

TV? Bertie skidded into the kitchen. He'd always wanted to be on TV and this could be his big chance!

"TV? Where? When?" he gabbled.

Dad groaned. He hadn't realized Bertie had been listening.

"This Saturday," he said. "But before you ask, I'm working so I can't take you."

"But it's *TV!*" said Bertie. "I'd be on TV!"

"I'm sure they'll get hundreds of boys applying," said Mum.

"Yes, but no one like ME!" argued Bertie.

"No, probably not," admitted Mum.

"Anyway, we don't know what it's for," said Dad. "It might just be a schools programme."

"Well I go to school, I'd be perfect!" said Bertie. "Pleeease!"

Dirty Bertie

"But who's going to take you?" asked
Mum. "I can't. Suzy's got a dance class."

"I've *got* to go, I can't miss this!"
wailed Bertie.

Mum had an idea. "What about Gran?
I suppose she might take him?"

"She might," said Dad.

"YESSSSS!" yelled Bertie, dancing
round the room. "I'm going to be on TV!"

Dirty Bertie

Gran thought a TV audition sounded
thrilling. She said she'd be delighted to
take Bertie. So on Saturday morning they
joined a long queue of boys and their
parents at Central Studios. Mum was
right – Bertie wasn't the only boy who
wanted to be on TV. He scowled at his
rivals, who were all dressed in their best
clothes. Their faces were scrubbed clean
and their hair shone like sunlight.

Dirty Bertie

Gran frowned at Bertie. "What's that on your face?" she said. "It looks like jam."

Bertie wriggled away as she tried to wipe it off with a tissue.

Gran sighed. Bertie looked as grubby and scruffy as ever.

"I wonder what sort of part it is," she said. "Maybe they'll want you to sing."

"Let's hope not," grunted Bertie. People usually covered their ears when he sang. But he did have acting experience. Last Christmas he'd played a dog in the musical *Oliver!* Everyone said it was a brilliant performance – apart from the bit when he'd brought down the scenery, but that could have happened to anyone.

CHAPTER 2

Two hours later, it was finally Bertie's turn to audition. They were shown into a room to meet Amy the director and her assistant, Paul.

"So, who have we got next?" asked Paul, checking his list. "Benny?"

"*Bertie*," said Bertie.

"What kind of TV show is it?" asked

Gran excitedly.

"It's an advert actually," explained Paul.

An *advert*! Bertie thought he'd be brilliant – he knew loads of adverts off by heart! And if it was an advert for sweets or chocolate he was willing to eat loads of them.

"I've done acting," he said. "I played a dog." He stuck out his tongue and panted, doing his best dog impression.

"Very good," said Amy. "But what we want is a boy who can be himself on camera."

"*I* can be myself," said Bertie. He was himself all the time – although usually it got him into trouble.

"Great," said Amy. She noticed Bertie's jam-stained face and wild hair. "Actually, you might suit the part," she said. "You're not like all the others we've seen today. You don't mind getting wet, I suppose?"

Bertie shook his head. It seemed like an odd question. Maybe it was raining in the advert. Or perhaps he'd be standing on a ship? If they needed a pirate captain, Bertie could do a brilliant accent.

"Just stand right here and read this line to the camera," said Paul.

Bertie took up his position and stared at the card Paul was holding.

"Mon-ster Bobbles for little mon-sters," he read.

"It's 'Monster Bubbles'," said Amy. "Try it again, with a bit more expression."

Bertie shut one eye. "AHARRRR! Monster Bubbles for little monsters!" he cried.

The director frowned. "What's with the funny voice?" she asked.

"I was being a pirate," Bertie told her. "I thought it'd make it more interesting."

"There aren't any pirates in this," said Amy. "Just stick to your normal voice."

"Be yourself," Gran reminded him.

Bertie thought being a pirate would be better, but he said the line again.

Amy nodded. "Thanks, that's great."

"Perfect," said Paul.

Bertie blinked. *Was that it?* Didn't they want to hear his other impressions? He could do teachers – Miss Boot on the warpath, for instance.

"Did I get the part?" he asked.

"We'll let you know," said Paul, showing them to the door. "Thanks for coming."

Outside, Bertie turned to Gran. "Well, that went pretty well I think," he said.

"Yes," agreed Gran. "If they want a one-eyed pirate with jam on his face, you're a certainty."

Dirty Bertie

The following week Bertie arrived home from school to find Gran in the kitchen clutching a letter addressed to him. He tore open the envelope and read the first few lines.

"I GOT IT!" he yelled. "WAHOOO! I got the part!"

Suzy gaped. Gran hugged him. Dad looked like he might faint.

"Seriously?" he said.

"See for yourself," said Bertie, handing over the letter. There it was in black and white. The TV company wanted Bertie at the studios next Saturday to film the advert.

"I told you!" grinned Bertie. He didn't see why his family looked so surprised. The TV people obviously knew talent when they saw it.

"What kind of advert is it?" asked Mum.

"I'm not exactly sure," said Gran.

"If they chose Bertie, it must be for air freshener," scoffed Suzy.

"Very funny," said Bertie. "Just because you're too ugly for TV!"

Gran tried to remember. "It was something about bubbles," she said. "Maybe it's a fizzy drink?"

Dirty Bertie

"Brilliant!" said Bertie. He loved fizzy drinks and held the class record for the longest burp. Anyway, who cared what the advert was for! What mattered was that he was going to appear on TV. Wait till his friends heard about this – they were going to be mad with envy!

"YOU? On *TV*?" said Darren, the next day.

"In your dreams," said Eugene.

"It's true," insisted Bertie. "I went to this audition and they picked me for an advert."

"Course they did," jeered Darren. "And they're paying you a million pounds."

"Maybe," said Bertie. "But it'll definitely be on TV."

His friends stared at him. "Seriously? A real advert – on *television*?" said Eugene.

"That's what I keep telling you!" said Bertie.

"Wow!" said Darren. "So what kind of advert?"

Bertie shrugged. "Dunno. It's probably some sort of fizzy drink," he said.

"Cool!" said Darren. "You'll be famous."

"I know!" said Bertie, grinning. "*World* famous!"

Dirty Bertie

And this was just the beginning, he thought. When the advert went out, everyone would want his autograph. Miss Boot would have to call him "Sir". Know-All Nick would bow when Bertie walked into class. Being on TV was going to be the best thing that had ever happened to him!

CHAPTER 3

On Saturday morning Bertie and Gran arrived at the TV studios. Bertie was so excited he could hardly keep still. He had been practising fizzy pop burps all week.

A girl called Ellie met them and took them along to a dressing room. Bertie sat in a leather chair while she started work on his make-up.

"I did tell him to wash his face this morning," sighed Gran.

"Don't worry," laughed Ellie. "The dirtier the better."

She was smearing Bertie's face with mud-coloured make-up. He looked like he'd just crawled out of a bog.

Gran looked puzzled. "Isn't he supposed to look smart?" she asked.

"Not for *this* advert." Ellie smiled. "He's meant to be as filthy as possible, otherwise he wouldn't need a bath."

Bertie sat up in his seat. Had he heard right? "A BATH?" he said.

"Yes, the advert's for bubble bath, didn't they tell you?" asked Ellie.

Bertie blinked. *Bubble bath?* Of course … that's what "Monster Bubbles" meant!

But wait a minute … surely they didn't
expect him to…

"I'm not – you know – actually *in* the
bath?" he gulped.

"Of course!"
laughed Ellie. "But
don't worry,
there'll be
plenty of
bubbles to
cover you."

Bertie turned
pale. Why hadn't
anyone warned
him?

He couldn't
appear on TV *in the bath*! He wouldn't
be wearing socks or a vest … or
anything!

Dirty Bertie

Finally it was time for Bertie's big scene. He waited nervously as the bath was prepared.

"I don't see why you're making such a big fuss," sighed Gran. "You have baths at home."

"Not often," said Bertie. "And not on TV!"

"But there'll be lots of bubbles," said Gran. "No one's going to see anything!"

"They'll see ME!" moaned Bertie. "You do it, if it's so easy!"

"I don't think anyone wants to see me in the bath!" giggled Gran.

Amy came over. "Ready, Bertie?" she asked.

Bertie swallowed. He hadn't minded

acting the first scene. All he'd had to do
was walk in looking filthy from playing
football – that came naturally. It was the
bath scene he was dreading. Under his
bathrobe he wore a tiny pair of pink
pants. Ellie claimed no one would see
them.

"Couldn't I keep the dressing gown
on?" he begged.

"Not in the bath," said Amy. "What's
up? Don't tell me you're embarrassed?"

"Course not." Bertie blushed. He
looked at Gran for help, but she just
shrugged her shoulders. It was too late
to back out now.

"Come on," said Amy. "Just get in the
bath and say the line. It's simple!"

Easy for you to say, thought Bertie.
You're not wearing pink pants.

Dirty Bertie

"Right, stand by everyone!" called Amy.

The filming started. Bertie's TV mum ran the taps, making clouds of bubbles.

"And action, Bertie!" said Amy.

Bertie dropped the bathrobe. Taking a run, he dived into the bath head first…

Water flew everywhere, soaking Amy and all the camera crew.

SPLOOSH!

Dirty Bertie

"Monster-bubblesh for li'l monsters!" burbled Bertie, from beneath a mountain of suds.

Amy wiped her eye. "Right," she said. "Let's try that again shall we, Bertie? And this time can we actually see your face?"

CHAPTER 4

Weeks passed. Bertie hoped that his starring TV role had been forgotten. Perhaps the advert wasn't going to be shown after all? When his friends asked questions, he mumbled excuses and changed the subject. But one Friday it arrived – a letter from the TV company. Bertie opened it and groaned.

"What is it?" asked Mum.

"Er ... nothing," said Bertie.

"It can't be nothing, let me see," said Mum. She read through the letter.

"But that's fantastic, Bertie!" she said. "Your advert's going out on Friday."

Bertie nodded glumly.

"Well, aren't you pleased?" asked Mum. "You're going to be on TV!"

"Mmm," said Bertie. "I'm just not feeling too well."

He still hadn't told anyone the terrible truth about the advert. His family had no idea and nor did anyone at school. Only Gran knew – and he'd made her promise to keep it a secret.

"Well, I can't wait to see it," said Mum.

"Nor me," said Suzy. "My smelly little brother on TV! We should invite Gran round to watch."

"Yes, and the Nicelys, too," said Mum. "I'm sure Angela would love to see it."

"No, not Angela!" groaned Bertie. If she heard about it, the news would be all round school. He didn't want *anyone* to see the advert.

The following evening Bertie's lounge was crowded with people. Despite his protests, Mum had invited Gran, Darren, Eugene and the Nicelys from next door. They were all eager to see Bertie's big moment on TV.

Bertie felt sick. Just as he'd feared,

Angela had blabbed about it to everyone. Even Miss Boot was going to watch. He stared at the TV. Perhaps they'd got the date wrong? Or maybe a sudden power cut would save him. Actually, that wasn't a bad idea...

"Isn't it exciting!" said Mum.

"Who'd have thought it? Bertie on TV," said Dad.

"Aren't *you* excited, Bertie?" cooed Angela, moving closer to him.

"Not really," said Bertie, sneaking out a hand for the remote.

ZAP! The TV went blank.

"What's happened?" gasped Gran.

"Oh no, a power cut," sighed Bertie.

"It's not a power cut, you're sitting on the remote, you idiot," said Darren. "Give it here."

Dirty Bertie

"Get off!" cried Bertie. A brief tug-of-war broke out, ending with Mum grabbing the remote and turning the TV back on.

The adverts were just starting. Bertie could only watch through his fingers. "Please, please, don't let them show it," he prayed.

"This is it!" cried Gran.

Bertie peeped out. There he was on the screen, covered in mud and holding a football.

"So *that's* why they chose you!" said Mum.

The scene changed to the bathroom.

Taps were running as Bertie's TV mum poured in bubble bath.

Here it comes, thought Bertie.

ARGH! There he was, wearing nothing but bubbles! The camera zoomed in... "Monster Bubbles for little monsters!"

Darren fell about laughing. "Ha ha ha! You didn't say you were in the bath!"

"Hee hee! Bertie's in the nuddy!" sang Eugene.

"Shut up! I was wearing pants!" moaned Bertie, turning pink.

"Well, I think you did very well, Bertie," said Gran.

Angela nodded. "I thought you were fantastic!"

"Yes, and at least you got a bath," laughed Dad.

Dirty Bertie

Bertie zapped off the TV.

"Okay, you've all seen it," he groaned. "Now can we just forget about it?"

Suzy grinned. "I wouldn't count on it," she said. "Adverts are on every day – they could be showing it for months yet!"

MONTHS? Bertie looked horrified. This was terrible! He was never going on TV again – not even if they begged him!

CHAPTER 1

It was Saturday suppertime. Bertie was meant to be laying the table with Suzy. Dad came in carrying a large box.

"I thought I might go fishing tomorrow," he said.

Bertie looked up hopefully. "Fishing? Can I come?" he asked.

"YOU? You don't like fishing," said Dad.

Dirty Bertie

"I've never been," replied Bertie.

"Probably because your dad's never offered to take you," said Mum, folding her arms.

Dad raised his eyes to the ceiling. Taking Bertie anywhere was risky, but fishing was asking for trouble. He'd probably get covered in mud and fall in the river. Whatever happened, one thing was certain – if Bertie came along there wouldn't be a moment's peace.

"You'd probably find it boring," said Dad. "Most of the time it's just sitting around."

"But don't you catch fish?" asked Bertie.

"Sometimes – if you're lucky," admitted Dad.

"I'd be good at fishing," said Bertie. "Remember when we got that goldfish?"

Suzy rolled her eyes. "That was at the funfair," she said.

All the same, Bertie was keen to go fishing. It sounded dead easy – you just dangled a hook in the water and pulled out a fish. Anyone could do it! Besides, anything that involved worms and maggots was his idea of heaven!

"Fishing's not that simple," argued Dad. "You have to learn how to cast a line."

"Surely you can teach him that?" said Mum. "I'd have thought you'd *want* to take your son fishing."

"I bet *other* dads take their sons," grumbled Bertie. "I bet they're *glad* to take them."

"Anyway, it would be nice for the two of you to do something together," said Mum.

Dad knew when he was beaten. "All right, all right, I'll take him," he groaned.

"YESSSSS!" cheered Bertie. "Can I borrow your fishing rod?"

"Certainly not, you'll break it," snapped Dad. "You can borrow my old fishing net."

Bertie supposed a net was better than nothing. He opened Dad's fishing box and examined the tins and boxes. He picked one up and took off the lid.

"Woah! MAGGOTS!" he gasped.
"Look, there's millions of them!"

"EWWW!" shrieked Suzy.

"ARGH! TAKE THEM
AWAY!" screamed
Mum with a
shudder.

Dad grabbed
the tin and
closed the lid.
"For goodness'
sake, leave things
alone, Bertie!"
he cried.

Bertie shrugged. He
didn't see why everyone
was so touchy. It was only a few measly
maggots after all. He wasn't planning
on racing them on the kitchen table.

He wiped his nose on his sleeve.
Tomorrow would be his first ever
fishing trip and he couldn't wait. Maybe
he would catch a real whopper – an
octopus or a great white shark. Imagine
the look on his friends' faces if he
brought one of *those* into school!

CHAPTER 2

The next morning, Bertie found Dad in the kitchen making sandwiches.

"You're not even dressed!" Dad moaned, glancing at the clock. "We need to get going!"

"I haven't had breakfast yet," grumbled Bertie.

"Well hurry up," said Dad, handing

him a plate. "If we don't get there early, we won't get a good spot."

Bertie couldn't see why they were in such a hurry. It was only half past eight! In any case, the fish weren't going anywhere – they were probably still in bed.

Dad dropped a couple of slices of bread into the toaster.

"Can't I have cereal?" asked Bertie.

"NO!" said Dad. "Just hurry up!"

Later that morning they arrived at the riverbank. Dad was anxious to claim his favourite fishing spot before anyone else got there. Bertie helped him carry their bags and boxes down to the river. There were quite a few fishermen out already.

Dad halted. "I knew it!" he groaned. "Someone's pinched our spot!"

"Where?" asked Bertie.

"There, under the trees," said Dad, pointing. "I always go there."

Bertie could see a man and a boy, sitting with their rods. They were both wearing floppy green hats – even so, the boy looked oddly familiar.

"Can't we tell them to move?" asked Bertie.

"Don't be daft!" said Dad. "We'll just have to find somewhere else."

They chose a spot a little way along the river. Bertie grabbed his fishing net and scrambled down the bank.

"Where are you going?" asked Dad.

"To catch a fish!" replied Bertie.

"We haven't set up yet!" said Dad. "Help me unpack."

Dirty Bertie

Bertie sighed and clambered back up. He couldn't see why fishing needed so much stuff! There were hooks, reels and lines, not to mention tins of flies, worms and maggots.

He unfolded a chair. "*Now* can I go?" he begged.

"Fishing isn't something you can hurry," explained Dad. "It's all in the preparation. You can't just dive in and expect to catch a fish!"

Bertie didn't see why not.

He waded in with his net, until the water sloshed over the top of his wellies.

Dirty Bertie

"Oh no, not *you!*" said a reedy voice behind him.

Bertie swung round. Standing on the bank was Know-All Nick in a baggy coat and floppy green hat. Bertie stared open-mouthed. It was bad enough seeing Nick at school every day, without him turning up here.

"You've pinched our spot," complained Bertie.

"Tough luck! We were here first!" simpered Nick. "My dad *always* takes me fishing on Sundays."

"He must be bonkers," said Bertie. He was surprised that Nick wanted to go fishing, what with all the maggots and worms. At school Nick screamed if a fly came near him.

"My dad knows *everything* about fishing," bragged Nick. "We're going to catch a whopper!"

"Huh!" scoffed Bertie. "Fat chance!"

"That's what you think," said Nick. "*I've* got my own fishing rod!"

"Big deal," said Bertie. "I've got a net and that's better."

"I don't *think* so," sneered Nick. "You won't catch a flea with your smelly old net!"

"Want to bet?" said Bertie.

They were interrupted by their dads arriving. Nick's dad looked as pale and weedy as his son.

"I hope you two boys are getting on," he said.

"Of course," lied Nick. "Bertie was

just telling me that his net's better than my fishing rod."

"I don't know about that," laughed Nick's dad. "Have you done much fishing?"

"It's my first time," answered Bertie.

"Oh dear! Nicholas got his first fishing rod when he was five!" boasted Nick's dad.

Dirty Bertie

"Bertie's never been interested in fishing," said Dad.

"Yes, I have!" argued Bertie. "You never take me!"

Dad looked at the ground.

"Anyway, we'll leave you to it," chuckled Nick's dad. "Best of luck."

"Yes, let me know if you catch any tiddlers, Bertie. TEE HEE!" sniggered Nick.

Bertie watched them go. He would show that big know-all. He was going to catch the biggest fish in the river, then they'd see who was laughing.

CHAPTER 3

The river drifted slowly by. Bertie
shivered in the wind. They'd been sitting
for hours without any sign of a fish.

"Can't I go paddling?" he pleaded.

"No, I've told you," said Dad. "You'll
frighten the fish away."

"What fish? There aren't any!"
moaned Bertie.

"Of course there are. Have a little patience," said Dad.

Bertie slumped back in his chair. He'd expected fishing to be a lot more exciting. He wasn't allowed to do anything! He couldn't throw stones, climb a tree or even swish his net in the river in case it frightened the fish.

"Isn't it lunchtime?" he nagged.

"Stop asking! It's only twelve o'clock!" sighed Dad.

"That *is* lunchtime," said Bertie. "I only had three slices of toast for breakfast."

"Okay, one sandwich," sighed Dad. "But don't wolf down the whole lot."

Bertie found the lunch box and took a sandwich. He glanced back at Nick and his dad – they looked like two garden gnomes clutching their fishing rods.

Dirty Bertie

Obviously Nick hadn't caught anything yet or he would have come over to gloat. *I wonder what he's got for lunch?* thought Bertie, as Dad catapulted a shower of maggots into the river. Suddenly a brilliant idea popped into Bertie's head. Maybe Nick would like a sandwich – a special *surprise sandwich?*

Bertie bent over the fishing box.

"What are you after?" asked Dad.

"Nothing! Just looking," said Bertie. He waited until Dad turned back to the river, then quickly grabbed a tin from the box. Inside was a sea of wriggling maggots.

Bertie took another
sandwich and scooped
in some juicy maggots,
hiding them under a slice of
cheese. It still looked like any ordinary
sandwich. He popped it back in the
box. Know-All Nick was in for a squirmy
surprise.

Bertie took the lunch box over to Nick
at the river's edge.

"Yum, yum!" he said, munching loudly.

Know-All Nick glared. "Do you have to
do that?" he grumbled.

"Fishing makes you hungry," said Bertie.
"Cheese and pickle's my favourite!"

Nick sniffed. "We've brought our own
sandwiches – carrot salad," he said.

Dirty Bertie

"YUCK! Not as nice as this," said Bertie. "Go on, try one."

He offered the lunch box. Nick frowned. It wasn't like Bertie to share his food. What was he up to?

"Have one!" urged Bertie.

Nick considered. Two could play at this game. "Okay, thanks," he said, taking the top sandwich.

Here goes, thought Bertie. *Wait till you taste my special surprise ingredient. Squirmy wormy maggots! Yum!*

Nick opened his mouth.

"Wait, I can't eat all this," he said, holding out the sandwich to Bertie. "Why don't we share it?"

Bertie's face fell. "WHAT?"

"Half each," said Nick. "It's only fair." He tore the sandwich in two and handed half to Bertie. "Eat up!" he said.

Bertie gulped, caught in his own trap.

"What's the matter? I thought cheese and pickle was your favourite?" jeered Nick.

"Um, yes," said Bertie. "But you go first."

"Oh no, after *you*," Nick insisted.

Bertie turned white. There was nothing for it. His stomach heaved. He slowly raised the squirmy sandwich to his lips and opened his mouth…

"Go on," crowed Nick.

Dirty Bertie

"NICHOLAS! Lunchtime!" called Nick's dad.

Bertie breathed a sigh of relief.

Saved!

"Got to go," said Nick, handing back his half of the sandwich. "Here, you keep it."

Bertie stomped back to his dad. Rats! What a waste of a good sandwich! He put both halves back into the box and closed the lid. Maybe he'd get a chance to slip it into Nick's bag later...

CHAPTER 4

Dad was sipping a cup of coffee from his flask.

"How's your friend? Has he caught anything?" he asked.

"Know-All Nick? No chance!" snorted Bertie. He checked his own net, which he'd left lying in the shallows hoping a fish might jump into it. Empty. Bertie sighed.

He had to catch something before Smugface beat him to it.

"Right, let's have something to eat," said Dad. "Where's the lunch box?"

Bertie handed it over and got out some crisps. Dad took the top sandwich. "That's funny," he frowned. "Did you cut these in half?"

"No," said Bertie. He looked up. Wait! The maggot sandwich… Hadn't he put it back in the box?

"STOP!" yelled Bertie.

Too late. Dad took a bite. "What's the matter?" he asked.

Bertie shook his head. Dad chewed for a moment, then pulled a face.

"This tastes funny, sort of salty," he said. "I'm sure they were all cheese and pickle."

Dirty Bertie

"They were… I mean, they are," stammered Bertie.

But Dad had opened the sandwich to check inside. His eyes bulged. His tongue came out.

"MAGGOTS!" he croaked, clutching his throat. "It's got maggots in it!"

"Yikes!" said Bertie. "How did they get in there?"

Dad spat out the sandwich on the grass.

"PLUGH! UGH! BLECH!"

Honestly, thought Bertie, *it's only a few maggots.* Dad sounded as if he was dying.

"DID YOU DO THIS?" cried Dad, waving the half-eaten sandwich.

"M-ME?" said Bertie.

"Who else?" snapped Dad. "You put maggots in here, didn't you?"

Bertie looked guilty. "Not on purpose! It was meant for Nick!" he wailed. "How was I to know YOU were going to eat it?"

Dad hurled the maggot sandwich into the river with a howl of rage.

"That's it," he fumed. "I feel sick! We're going home."

"But Dad…" said Bertie.

"No buts, I knew this was a bad idea," said Dad.

"But Dad!" cried Bertie, pointing to the river. "LOOK!"

The maggot sandwich was bobbing around like a cork on the water. Dad jumped to his feet. It could only mean one thing…

"A FISH!" he yelled. "Quick! Where's my rod?"

But Bertie didn't wait. He sploshed into the river and plunged in his net. When he scooped it out, there was something flapping in the bottom – a big silver fish.

"WOW! A WHOPPER!" gasped Bertie.

Dirty Bertie

Dad helped him haul the fish into the shallows, where they emptied it into a larger net.

"That's a carp!" said Dad. "A monster, too!"

"I told you!" grinned Bertie. "I told you I'd catch one!"

The noise brought Nick and his dad running over. When Nick saw Bertie's prize catch, he could hardly believe it.

"You caught that?" he said. "But … but how?"

"With my smelly old net, how do you think?" said Bertie.

"Good heavens!" said Nick's dad, impressed.

"Beginner's luck," sneered Nick.

Dad shook his head. "Oh, I don't think luck had anything to do with it," he said.

Dirty Bertie

"No," grinned Bertie. "The secret of fishing is you just need the right sandwiches!"

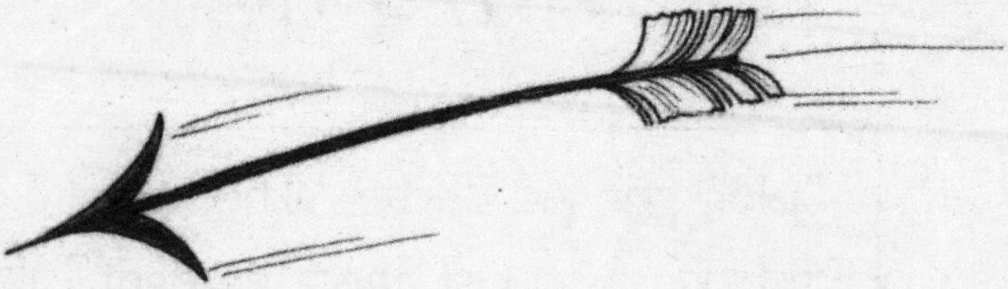

OUTLAW!

CHAPTER 1

TWANG!

Bertie's imaginary bow sent an arrow winging into the sky. He was Robin Hood, the fearless outlaw, wanted dead or alive. This morning Miss Boot had read to her class from *The Tales of Robin Hood,* and for once Bertie had stopped yawning and listened. Robin Hood lived in the forest with his merry men and spent his time robbing the rich to give to the poor. This was the life, thought Bertie – he was *born* to lead a gang of outlaws.

Dirty Bertie

"Follow me, men!" he cried. "Let's find someone rich who wants robbing!"

"Okay, Robin!" said Darren-the-Dale.

"Who shall we ambush?" asked Eugene Scarlet.

Bertie looked around the playground for a likely victim. Over on a bench sat a pale-faced boy munching an apple. Aha! The evil Sheriff of Nickingham – Know-All Nick! The outlaws crept closer, silent as mice. On Bertie's signal, they leaped out, taking aim with their imaginary bows and arrows.

"SURRENDER!" yelled Bertie.

Know-All Nick almost choked on his apple. "URGH! Heeelp!" he squawked.

"I am Robin Hood," cried Bertie. "And these are my brave outlaws. Turn out your pockets!"

"Push off!" said Know-All Nick.

"Right, don't say we didn't warn you," said Bertie. "Take him prisoner, men."

Nick leaped to his feet. "You touch me and I'll scream," he warned. "Miss Boot doesn't like fighting in the playground."

Bertie frowned. He knew Miss Boot was on playground patrol today and Nick's screams would bring her running. Rats! Maybe they'd have to rob the cowardly sheriff another day...

Dirty Bertie

Over by the fence, Angela Nicely was skipping with her friends. The outlaws sneaked up behind them.

"YAHAAAAA! SURRENDER!" yelled Bertie.

Angela stopped skipping. "Hello, Bertie. Are you playing pirates?"

"Course not. I'm Robin Hood and we are the outlaws of Sherbet Forest," said Bertie.

Angela clapped her hands. "Goodie! Can *I* be Robin Hood?" she begged.

"No chance," said Bertie. "There's only one Robin Hood and that's me. We arm-wrestled for it and I won."

"Okay then, I'll be an outlaw," offered Angela.

"You can't," said Bertie. "We don't have girls in our gang."

Dirty Bertie

Angela stepped a little closer, fluttering her eyelashes.

"Pleeease, Bertie!" she cooed.

Bertie gulped. He hadn't forgotten the time Angela had chased him round the playground trying to kiss him. What if she did it again in front of his friends? There was only one thing to do…

"RUN!" cried Bertie.

Dirty Bertie

The brave outlaws fled round the corner.

"This is hopeless," panted Bertie. "I bet Robin Hood never had this trouble."

"Maybe we should take it in turns robbing each other?" suggested Eugene.

"That's no good, we've got to rob the rich – that's what they did in the story," argued Darren.

"Exactly," agreed Bertie. "There's got to be *someone* worth robbing."

He looked around, trying to think. "I know – Royston Rich!" he cried. Royston was the biggest show off in the class. He came to school every day in his dad's sports car and he was always bragging about the swimming pool in his garden. If anyone deserved to be set on by outlaws it was Royston!

CHAPTER 2

Bertie and his gang sneaked across the playground. They found Royston behind the boys' toilets, cramming a chocolate bar into his mouth. On Bertie's signal, the outlaws jumped out.

"HANDS UP! SURRENDER!" yelled Bertie, waving a stick he'd picked up.

Royston wiped his mouth. "What do

you want?" he groaned.

"We're outlaws," Darren told him.

"You fooled me," jeered Royston.

"Well, I'm Robin Hood and this is a robbery," said Bertie. "Hand over your gold."

"I don't have any gold, stupid," replied Royston.

"Then hand over your chocolate," said Darren.

"Please," added Eugene.

"Or else," said Bertie.

Royston folded his arms. "Or else what?" he said. "You're all going to wet your pants?"

Bertie poked his stick into Royston's chest. But Royston grabbed it and snapped the stick in half, throwing it on the ground.

"Huh! Some outlaws you are," he sneered. "You couldn't rob my little sister!" He walked off, treading on Bertie's foot as he passed.

"That went well," said Eugene.

"Why didn't you stop him?" grumbled Bertie.

"You're Robin Hood, *you* stop him," said Darren.

Bertie rolled his eyes. This was getting them nowhere – Know-All Nick had got away, Angela had tried to join them and now Royston Rich had made them look stupid! How could they be outlaws if they couldn't manage a simple robbery?

"We'll get him later," said Bertie. "He always goes to the sweet shop after school. We'll wait outside and nab his sweets."

Eugene frowned. "Can't we be good outlaws?" he asked. "My mum says it's wrong to steal."

"It's not stealing, it's robbing the rich," said Bertie.

"Same thing," said Eugene.

"No, it's not," argued Bertie. "Robin

Hood robbed the rich and Miss Boot
said he's a legend."

"Yes," said Eugene, "but he gave to
the poor."

"That's what we're doing, too," said
Bertie. "Royston's loaded and he always
has tons of sweets. We're just helping
him to share them out."

"Exactly," said Darren. "That way it's
fairer for everyone."

Eugene shrugged. When you put it
like that, it was hard to argue. "But what
if we get caught?" he worried.

"We won't," said Bertie. "We'll
disguise ourselves as outlaws so he
won't know who we are."

CHAPTER 3

After school the outlaws hurried to the sweet shop. They hid behind a wall and waited for Royston Rich to appear. All three had hankies tied over their faces, which Bertie claimed was an old outlaw trick.

"Here he comes," whispered Darren. "Keep down."

Dirty Bertie

Royston pushed open the door
and went into the sweet shop. A few
minutes later, he came out clasping
a bag and cramming sweets into his
mouth three at a time.

"Now!" whispered Bertie.

"YAHAAAAA!" The masked outlaws
swarmed forward, surrounding Royston.

"Surrender or die!" yelled Bertie.

Dirty Bertie

Royston clutched the bag to his chest. The leader of the outlaws had a dirty face half hidden by a grubby hanky. It could only be one person.

"Bertie!" cried Royston.

"No, it's not," lied Bertie. "Hand over the sweets."

"No way," said Royston. "I'm not scared of you lot."

"Okay, you asked for it," said Bertie. "Tickle him!"

The outlaws advanced, fingers at the ready.

"No, please! I'm not ticklish!" squawked Royston, backing away. "Ha ha! Hee hee!"

He squirmed and wriggled, dropping the bag of sweets on the ground.

Bertie scooped it up, waving the bag in the air.

"Got it!" he cried. "Come on, men, back to Sherbet Forest!"

The outlaws ran off down the road, whooping in triumph.

"I'll get you for this, Bertie!" howled Royston. "I'm telling on you!"

Dirty Bertie

Back at the park, the outlaws hid in their secret forest camp near the playground.

Eugene looked around anxiously. "Now we're for it," he said. "Royston knows who we are."

"Stop worrying," said Bertie. "Have a liquorice torpedo."

They all helped themselves from Royston's bag.

"So anyway, who shall we share them with?" asked Eugene.

"*Share* them?" said Darren.

"Yes, you know, robbing the rich to give to the poor," Eugene reminded them. "Like Robin Hood."

"That's right," said Bertie, sucking a lemon sherbet. "If we're going to be outlaws we've got to do it properly. The question is, who deserves a share of the sweets?"

"What about Donna?" suggested Darren.

"She's not poor!" scoffed Bertie.

"Trevor then."

"He's a vegetarian, they don't eat sweets," said Darren.

"Well, who then?" asked Eugene.

Bertie frowned. It was complicated. If they shared the sweets with one of their friends, then it wasn't fair on all the others. They could always divide them equally – but then there wouldn't be enough to go round.

"Let's go back to my house," suggested Bertie. "We can decide later."

The outlaws agreed that this was a

Dirty Bertie

good plan and set off, passing round
the sweets as they went.

Ten minutes later they reached Bertie's
house and paused at the gate.

"Better hide the bag," warned Darren.
"Your mum will ask where we got all
these sweets."

"Good thinking," said Bertie,
but looking in the bag,
his face fell. "There's not
that many left," he said.

"WHAT? How many?"
asked Eugene.

Bertie counted. "Four."

"FOUR!" cried Darren.
"That can't be right – who's
scoffed them all?"

"I guess we did," admitted Bertie.

They had certainly helped themselves to one or two sweets at the park … then one or two more on the way home. Possibly it might have been six or seven.

Eugene rolled his eyes. "But what about sharing them with the poor?" he moaned.

"Four sweets aren't going to go far," said Bertie.

"No," agreed Darren. "Four's hardly worth keeping."

Bertie emptied them out into his hand.

"Might as well eat them," he said. "One each and I'll save one for Whiffer."

They finished off the last of the sweets. On the whole Bertie thought they'd acted pretty fairly. He was almost certain Robin Hood would have done the same thing.

CHAPTER 4

Next morning, the three outlaws trooped into school. Royston Rich was waiting for them in the playground.

"Right, fat face, where's my sweets?" he demanded.

Bertie frowned. "What sweets?" he asked.

"You know what sweets – the ones

you stole from me yesterday," said
Royston. "If I don't get them back, I'm
telling Miss Boot."

"You wouldn't!" said Eugene.

"Just watch me," said Royston.

They filed into class. A minute
later Miss Boot swept into the room,
scattering the class to their desks.

"Sit down and no talking," she barked.

Royston gave Bertie a
goofy smile. He stood up
and raised his hand.

Uh oh, now we're for it,
thought Bertie.

"Miss Boot," whined
Royston. "Bertie and his
friends took my sweets!"

"I said, 'NO talking'!"
snapped Miss Boot.

Dirty Bertie

"But Miss—" began Royston.

"QUIET!" boomed Miss Boot. "I am not interested in silly tales about sweets. I've told you before you're NOT to bring them to school. Anyone caught eating sweets will have me to deal with. DO I MAKE MYSELF CLEAR?"

Royston nodded and sat down sulkily. He scowled at Bertie. This wasn't over yet – not by a long way.

At break time Bertie and his friends charged out into the playground. Royston marched up to them.

"Fat lot of good that did," crowed Bertie. "Serves you right for telling tales."

"Never mind that," said Royston. "You've got to help me."

Checking that no one was looking, he brought out a paper bag. Inside were three pale blue gobstoppers, as big as golf balls.

"Where did you get those?" gasped Darren.

"From the sweet shop this morning," said Royston. "But what am I going to do? You heard what Miss Boot said – no sweets in school."

"I'd hate to be in your shoes if she catches you," said Eugene. "Better hide them quickly."

"Yes, but *where*?" moaned Royston.

Bertie eyed the gobstoppers and licked his lips. This was too good to be true.

"We could hide them for you if you like," he offered.

"*Really?* Would you?" said Royston gratefully.

Bertie shrugged. "No problem," he said. "I'm sure we'll think of something."

"Anything!" said Royston. "Just don't let Miss Boot see them or I'm dead!"

He handed over the bag and hurried off, looking pleased with himself.

"Are you mad?" Darren asked Bertie. "Where are we going to hide three huge gobstoppers?"

Bertie raised his eyebrows. "Where do you think?" he said, reaching into the bag.

When the bell went they all trooped back into class. Royston Rich turned round and gave Bertie a goofy grin. Bertie frowned. He didn't see what Royston was so pleased about. He wouldn't be seeing those giant gobstoppers again.

But as the lesson started, Bertie noticed that the three of them were attracting some funny looks. *What was going on?*

He nudged Darren. "Have I got something on my face?" he whispered.

Darren looked at him. "YIKES! Your lips – they're bright blue!" he hissed.

Dirty Bertie

Bertie stared. "So are yours!" he gasped. "And Eugene's, too!"

All three of them had bright blue lips with blue tongues to match. They looked like weird aliens! But how had it happened? Bertie groaned. The gobstoppers! That sneaky rat Royston had tricked them into eating joke sweets. If Miss Boot ever found out, they were in BIG trouble. Bertie slid down in his seat.

"BERTIE!" barked Miss Boot. "SIT UP STRAIGHT! What are you doing?"

"Nuffink!" mumbled Bertie.

"Speak up!" snapped Miss Boot. "And take your hand away from your mouth when you're talking."

Slowly Bertie removed his hand. Miss Boot stared at his bright blue lips. Then she noticed Darren and Eugene.

Dirty Bertie

There could only be one explanation…

"SWEETS!" thundered Miss Boot. "You've been eating sweets! Come out to the front, all of you!"

Bertie groaned. They'd probably be picking up litter in the playground for the rest of their lives. That did it, he thought. No more Robin Hood or robbing the rich. Starting tomorrow he was going back to the quiet life of a pirate.